SkippyjonJones

CIRQUE DE OLÉ

JUDY SCHACHNER

DIAL BOOKS FOR YOUNG READERS
AN IMPRINT OF PENGUIN GROUP (USA) INC.

To Los Poochitos de la Triple T.P.:
Mario, Felipé, Noel, Yasmin, Matthew, Matteo, and Halecita —
And in memory of little Leo Zenk
Love, Judy

Gracias to Pina, the biggest of the small ones,
and Ginger and Javier

DIAL BOOKS FOR YOUNG READERS
A division of Penguin Young Readers Group

PUBLISHED BY THE PENGUIN GROUP

Penguin Group (USA) Inc., 375 Hudson Street, New York, New York 10014, U.S.A. ● Penguin Group (Canada), 90 Eglinton Avenue East, Suite 700, Toronto, Ontario M4P 2Y3, Canada (a division of Pearson Penguin Canada Inc.) ● Penguin Books Ltd, 80 Strand, London WC2R 0RL, England ● Penguin Ireland, 25 St Stephen's Green, Dublin 2, Ireland (a division of Penguin Books Ltd) ● Penguin Group (Australia), 250 Camberwell Road, Camberwell, Victoria 3124, Australia (a division of Pearson Australia Group Pty Ltd) ● Penguin Books India Pvt Ltd, 11 Community Centre, Panchsheel Park, New Delhi - 110 017, India ● Penguin Group (NZ), 67 Apollo Drive, Rosedale, Auckland 0632, New Zealand (a division of Pearson New Zealand Ltd) ● Penguin Books (South Africa) (Pty) Ltd, 24 Sturdee Avenue, Rosebank, Johannesburg 2196, South Africa ● Penguin Books Ltd, Registered Offices: 80 Strand, London WC2R 0RL, England

Library of Congress Cataloging-in-Publication Data
Schachner, Judith Byron Skippyjon Jones Cirque de Olé / by Judy Schachner. p. cm.
Summary: Skippyjon Jones, the Siamese cat that thinks he is a Chihuahua dog, wants to perform his high-wire act in the circus. ISBN 978-0-8037-3782-2 (hardcover) [1. Siamese cat—Fiction. 2. Cats—Fiction. 3. Chihuahua (Dog breed)—Fiction. 4. Dogs—Fiction. 5. Circus—Fiction. 6. Acrobats—Fiction.] I. Title. II. Title: Cirque de Olé.
PZ7.S3286Sjj 2012   [E]—dc23   2012012075

Published in the United States by Dial Books for Young Readers,
a division of Penguin Young Readers Group, 345 Hudson Street, New York, New York 10014
www.penguin.com/youngreaders

Designed by Heather Wood
1 2 3 4 5 6 7 8 9 10 ● First Edition ● Manufactured in China

The illustrations for this book were created in acrylics and pen and ink on Aquarelle Arches watercolor paper.

Skippyjon Jones was a
real High-Wire Henry.

And that made his mama as worried as a worm in a wading pool.

"Oh, my fleas," wailed Mama Junebug Jones. "Come down from that wire before you break all your bones!"

"He can't hear you," sang his sisters, Ju-Ju Bee, Jezebel, and Jilly Boo, "'cause Skippy's up in squirrely world."

The girls were right. The kitty boy was performing tail-tingling tricks on the telephone wire above them.

"That's amazing," gushed the girls. "He should join the circus."

"Circus berserkus!" groaned Mama. "I'm calling the Fire Department."

"Fire Department?" repeated Jilly Boo. "Skippy's not on fire, he's on wire."

But before Junebug Jones could press a button, the kitty boy did a triple-spin backflip dive right into Mama's apron pocket.

"That was really good for a Chi-wu-lu," said Ju-Ju Bee.

"The word is *Chihuahua*," said Mama, frazzled. "And he is not that. Skippyjon Jones is a Siamese cat."

Then she lugged her catch of the day back to his room for a time-out and a big talk.

"What did you think you were doing up there? *You* and *those squirrels* on a *wire* in *midair?* What if you **tripped** and fell on your head? You'd have to spend **months** in a hospital bed!"

Then, as Junebug Jones pawed at her hives, she let the truth slip about cats and nine lives.

"I wish we had nine, but we only have one. So think about that, my Siamese son."

Then she closed the door.

The kitty boy was thinking all right . . . about bouncing on his big-boy bed.

"Oh, I'm **Skippyjonjones**,

And I don't have nine lives.

"So what's the big deal?

Hey, did I just see flies?"

Indeed he did, and he chased
one over to his mirror. . . .

Where he ate it.

"Holy snack-ito!" exclaimed the kitty boy. "Love 'dem crunchies."

Then he looked into the mirror and, using his very best Spanish accent, he said, "If I have but one life to live, *muchacho*, let me live it as a Chihuahua."

In less time than it takes a flea to fly to Florida, Skippyjon Jones put together a fine costume while he sang in a *muy, muy* soft voice.

"Oh, my name is Skippito Friskito, (clap-clap)

And I'm one handsome daredevil-ito.

I'm physically fit, (clap-clap)

Every part, every bit,

Just right for a circus pooch-ito." (clap-clap)

In the meantime, over in the sewing nook, Mama was attempting to have a sensible conversation with the girls.

"Where is Jilly Boo's tutu?"
asked Mama.

"The Chi-wu-lu has the tutu,"
replied Ju-Ju Bee.

"Whatever for?"
asked Mama.

"Because Chi-wu-lus
wear tutus," said Jezebel.

"And cows wear muumuus,"
added Ju-Ju Bee.

"And boo-boos wear Band-Aids,"
continued Jezebel.

"And I need a nap!"
moaned Mama.

But the Chi-wu-lu wasn't thinking tutus, muumuus, or boo-boos. He was thinking of flying through the air with the greatest of fleas . . . just like the dog on a flying trapeze.

Until *thump*, he planted his paws in a purr-fecto landing on the turf outside the *Cirque de* . . .

"¡Olé!" shouted his *amigos*, *los Chimichangos*.

"Hola!" hollered back Skippito Friskito, the great acrobat-ito, to his barking buddies.

"Hold your ponies, puppito," declared Poquito Tito, the smallest of the small ones. "Have you grown a *bigote*?"

"No, I did not grow a mustache-ito," answered the *gatito*. "It's just part of my costume."

"¡Bueno!" said Don Diego, the biggest of the small ones. "Because we need you to grow something **mucho _más_ _importante_**."

PERFORMING FLEAS ALIVE

"But what can be more important than a mustache, _muchachos_?" asked Skippito.

"¡*Los músculos!*" said all the puppitos.

"Not the lump-itos *giganticos*?" declared Skippito.

"Oh *sí, muchacho*," said Poquito Tito. "The muscles."

Then Don Diego pulled an old circus poster out of his right ear and let it unroll.

"Now do you get it, dude?"

THE
FIRST TIME
IN AMERICA
TINGLING
BROS
AND
CIRQUE de OLÉ PRESENTS
THE TINY
Trembling
TOWER
OF TOWER

"Oh, I get it all right,"
said Skippito. "It means I am
low dog on the totem pole."

This made the Chihuahuas
twist and shout.

"Oh yes, that's right, Skippito, (clap-clap)

Your cabeza is just what we need-o. (clap-clap)

And your muscles must grow,

Just in time for the show,

Or else we will all crumble-ito."

(clap-clap)

Then all the *perritos* snuck under the skirts of the big top.

First the *muchachos* tippytoed by the *caballista* practicing on her pony.

Then they slipped past the *payaso*, putting his paper-popping puppy through his paces.

But it wasn't until they reached the *elefante* that the puppitos had to worry.

"Watch your step, *amigos*," warned Poquito Tito. "We are but *pulgas* to her."

"We are not fleas," said Skippito. "We are Chihuahuas!"

And that wasn't all the doggies
had to watch out for.

They saw *léones* and *tigres* and *osos*. Oh, my!

PUTZI SHTRUNGLEBOOT THE SHTRONGDOG 80 lbs of MEAN MAD MUSCLE with a MEATBALL for a BRAIN

Sensational

But the most dangerous animal of all lay sleeping like a baby in his cage. "Let's take a peek, puppitos," said Skippito.

"Let's just take his *traje*," suggested Poquito Tito.

"Not his costume!" declared Skippito, alarmed. "*¿Por qué?*"

"Because it will look *mucho major* on you, señor."

Then they raced like rabbits over to their dressing room.

But the circus
waits for no dog. So with
the speed of a spitball, the
poochitos changed their *chico*
into a world-class circus *perro
con músculos.*

First they gave him a *vitamina.*
Then they pulled on his new *traje.*

"It's too big,"
complained the *gatito.*

"No worries,"
woofed Don Diego.

"We will PUMP YOU UP."

And pump the *perros* did, singing,

"Oom-pah-pah, loom-pah-pah-lito,

(clap-clap)

We'll give you the muscles you need-o,

(clap-clap)

Cuz strong you must be,

For the triple T.P.,

So we don't all go

BOOM

tumble-ito."

(clap-clap)

Then it was
the moment of truth
as they floated Skippito
out under the big top.

Perros poured out from every point and piled on top of Skippito's *grande cabeza.*

UP, UP UP
they climbed until they formed a *perfecto* tower of tiny, trembling Chihuahuas.

And beneath the tower stood the power, tough and shaky as five-day-old Jell-O.

But just as the pups were about to make circus history . . .

Putzi Shtrungleboot, the
Shtrong Dog, strutted
out into the center ring
and bit the behind of
his very own *traje*.

"*¡Olé!*"
shouted the crowd.

"Oh no!"
cried Skippito as the tiny
Trembling Tower of Power
tumbled from his head.

TA-DA!

blasted *la banda* as Skippito flew up
into the rafters like a punctured balloon.

"Whoohoo!"

hooted the crowd as the *gatito*
caught hold of *el trapecio*. Then
he flew through the air with the
greatest of squeeze—

—the brave little cat on the flying trapeze. But just as he reached the highest point, Skippito let go and dazzled the audience again with a double twirly-squirrely twist onto the tightrope.

But the tightrope acted just like a slingshot, and

Thwappppp!

It sent Skippito Up Up Up to the tippety top of the tent.

Then *Shoooooop!*

Down
Down
Down he dove, *cabeza* first into the cotton candy kitten ball cannon.

Where Putzi Shtrungleboot, the Shtrong Dog, was waiting to light the fuse.

"Drumroll, *por favor!*" ordered Don Diego.

-but-ta-but-ta-but-ta-but-ta-but-ta-but-ta-but-ta-

Then

KA-BOOM!!

El Skippito Friskito, the great acrobat-ito, blasted out of the circus, out of his closet, and right out of his room.

"SMACK-A-DOODLE-DOO!" shouted the kitty boy as he collided with his mama's head.

"Wow!" exclaimed Jezebel. "Where did he come from?"

"He came from the circus, silly," said Jilly Boo.

Later that night, after a piece of maple mouse pie, the kitty boy made up a rhyme just for his mama and delivered it with a most sincere bounce.

"Oh, I'm Skippyjonjones,

But you're the bees' knees,

'Cuz your cookin' is smokin'—"

"Hey, did I just see fleas?" asked Mama, beginning to scratch.

"Circus fleas," replied the kitty boy proudly.

"Circus berserkus," muttered Mama. "Get your collars out, kittens. It's going to be an itchy night."